# Biking

## A Level Two Reader

By Cynthia Klingel and Robert B. Noyed

Every kid loves to ride a bike.

It is time to get a new bike!

The bike shop is full of new bikes. Mr. Ryan puts together the bikes when they come into the store.

There are many parts to a bike. Mr. Ryan knows how to fit the parts together.

Mr. Ryan puts on the wheels and the chain. He adds the seat, the handlebars, and the kickstand.

Mr. Ryan checks the brakes. He makes sure the bike is ready to ride. The bike looks great.

You put on your helmet. You leave to ride to the park.

13

You stop at the stoplight

and wait to cross the street.

At the park, you ride up the hill. It is hard work to pedal. You change gears to make it easier.

18

The bike goes very fast. You ride down the hill.

This is a great bike. This is the bike for you!

# Index

# To Find Out More

## Books

Erlbach, Arlene, and Jackie Urbanovic (illustrator). *Bicycles.* Minneapolis, Minn.: Lerner Publications Co., 1994

Gibbons, Gail. *The Bicycle Book.* New York: Holiday House, 1999.

Loewen, Nancy, and Penny Dann (illustrator). *Bicycle Safety.* Chanhassen, Minn.: The Child's World, 1997.

## Web Sites

### National Bicycle History Archive of America
*http://members.aol.com/oldbicycle/index.html*
Details about the history of bicycles as well as information about restoration.

### Ride Safe
*http://ridesafeinc.com/index.html*
A site dedicated to bike safety and helmet information.

# Note to Parents and Educators

Welcome to The Wonders of Reading™! These books provide text at three different levels for beginning readers to practice and strengthen their reading skills. Additionally, the use of nonfiction text provides readers the valuable opportunity to *read to learn*, not just to learn to read.

These leveled readers allow children to choose books at their level of reading confidence and performance. Level One books offer beginning readers simple language, word choice, and sentence structure as well as a word list. Level Two books feature slightly more difficult vocabulary, longer sentences, and longer total text. In the back of each Level Two book are an index and a list of books and Web sites for finding out more information. Level Three books continue to extend word choice and length of text. In the back of each Level Three book are a glossary, an index, and a list of books and Web sites for further research.

State and national standards in reading and language arts emphasize using nonfiction at all levels of reading development. The Wonders of Reading™ fill the historical void in nonfiction material for the primary grade readers with the additional benefit of a leveled text.

# About the Authors

Cindy Klingel has worked as a high school English teacher and an elementary teacher. She is currently the curriculum director for a Minnesota school district. Writing children's books is another way for her to continue her passion for sharing the written word with children. Cindy Klingel is a frequent visitor to the children's section of bookstores and enjoys spending time with her many friends, family, and two daughters.

Bob Noyed started his career as a newspaper reporter. Since then, he has worked in communications and public relations for more than fourteen years for a Minnesota school district. He enjoys writing books for children and finds that it brings a different feeling of challenge and accomplishment from other writing projects. He is an avid reader who also enjoys music, theater, traveling, and spending time with his wife, son, and daughter.

Readers should remember...
All sports carry a certain amount of risk. To reduce your risk while biking, bike at your own experience level, wear all safety equipment, and use care and common sense. The publisher and author will take no responsibility or liability for injuries resulting from bike riding.

**Published by The Child's World®, Inc.**
PO Box 326
Chanhassen, MN  55317-0326
800-599-READ
www.childsworld.com

With special thanks to the Kersten Family and the Edgebrook Cycle and Sport Shop for providing the modeling and location for this book.

**Photo Credits**
All photos © Flanagan Publishing Services/Romie Flanagan

Project Coordination: Editorial Directions, Inc.
Photo Research: Alice K. Flanagan

**Library of Congress Cataloging-in-Publication Data**
Klingel, Cynthia Fitterer.
Biking / by Cynthia Klingel and Robert B. Noyed.
p.   cm.  —  (Wonder books)
"A level 2 reader" —Cover.
Includes bibliographical references (p. ) and index.
Summary: Illustrations and simple text describe the fun a child has riding a new bicycle.
ISBN 1-56766-815-1 (library reinforced : alk. paper)
1. Cycling—Juvenile literature.   [1. Cycling.]
I. Noyed, Robert B.   II. Title.   III. Wonder books (Chanhassen, Minn.)

GV1043.5 .K45          2000
796.6—dc21             99-057407